A **Rookie reader**

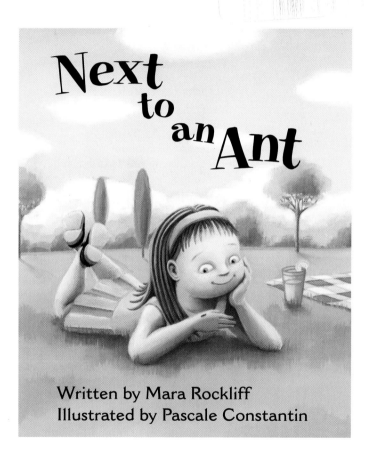

Next to an Ant

Written by Mara Rockliff
Illustrated by Pascale Constantin

SCHOLASTIC INC.

New York   Toronto   London   Auckland   Sydney
Mexico City   New Delhi   Hong Kong   Buenos Aires

For Cassidy
—M.R.

In memory of lovely picnics on the mountain with Nathalie and Patrick
—P.C.

Reading Consultants

Linda Cornwell
Literacy Specialist

Katharine A. Kane
Education Consultant
(Retired, San Diego County Office of Education
and San Diego State University)

ISBN 0-516-25237-2

12 11 10 9 8 7 6 5 4 3 2 1   5 6 7 8 9 10/0

Printed in the U.S.A.   61

First Scholastic paperback printing, March 2005

Next to an ant,
a berry is tall.

Next to a berry,
a snail is tall.

Next to a snail,
a mouse is tall.

Next to a mouse,
my shoe is tall.

Next to my shoe,
my cup is tall.

Next to my cup,
my ball is tall.

Next to my ball,
my basket is tall.

Next to my basket,
my puppy is tall.

Next to my puppy,
my brother is tall.

And I?

I am the tallest one of all!

Word List (25 words)

a	brother	puppy
all	cup	shoe
am	I	snail
an	is	tall
and	mouse	tallest
ant	my	the
ball	next	to
basket	of	
berry	one	

About the Author

Next to an ant, Mara Rockliff is very tall indeed. She lives in Charlottesville, Virginia, with her family.

About the Illustrator

Pascale Constantin was born in Montreal, cultural center of French-speaking Canada. She chose art over hockey at a young age, taking to it like a duck out of water. After many years as a sculptor, Pascale discovered a passion for illustration. Fantastic creatures and funny characters jump from her brushes onto the paper as if by magic. She currently lives in Barbados with her husband, David, and their two very naughty dogs, Lulu and Thor.